Knights Taste Terrible!

Maverick Early Readers

'Knights Taste Terrible!'
An original concept by Rebecca Colby
© Rebecca Colby 2021

Illustrated by Katie Kear

Published by MAVERICK ARTS PUBLISHING LTD
Studio 11, City Business Centre, 6 Brighton Road,
Horsham, West Sussex, RH13 5BB
© Maverick Arts Publishing Limited November 2021
+44 (0)1403 256941

A CIP catalogue record for this book is available at the British Library.

ISBN 978-1-84886-832-8

Maverick
publishing
www.maverickbooks.co.uk

Orange
This book is rated as: Orange Band (Guided Reading)
It follows the requirements for Phase 5 phonics.
Most words are decodable, and any non-decodable words are familiar, supported by the context and/or represented in the artwork.

Knights Taste Terrible!

by
Rebecca Colby

illustrated by
Katie Kear

Viktor was trapped again.

Each time he went into the woods, he met a dragon. And each time he met a dragon, it tried to eat him.

"Not again," said Viktor.

"I need a new job."

"You look plump and yummy," said the dragon.

"No," said Viktor. "Knights taste terrible. Let me make a nice chicken soup for you."

"I like chicken," said the dragon, "but I'm hungry now. I need to eat."

The dragon picked up Viktor and licked his lips.

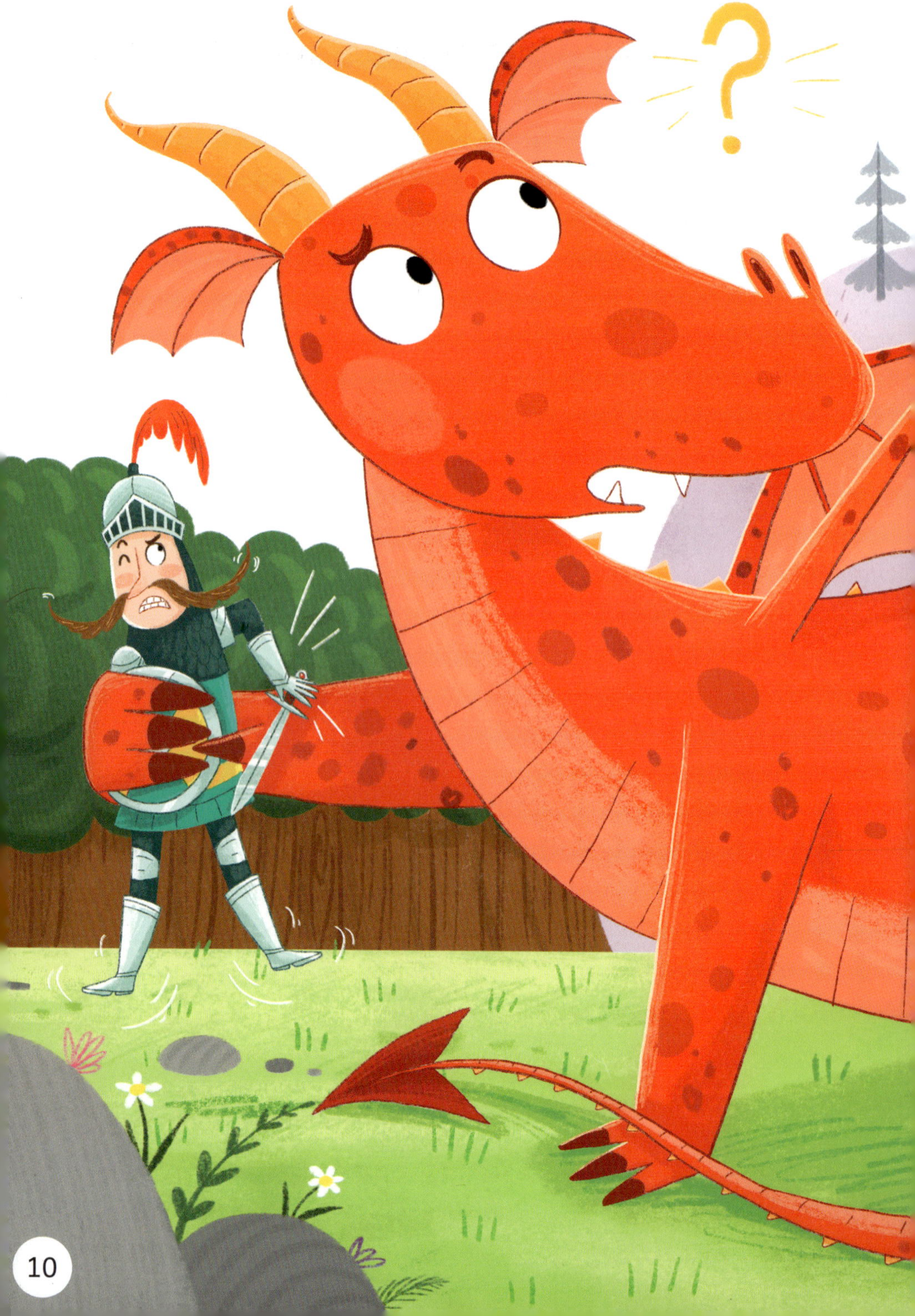

But the dragon had never eaten a knight.

He didn't know how. So Viktor tricked him.

"Let me help you," said Viktor.

"Eat this first. It's the best part."

The dragon looked at the small, pointy thing. He took a bite.

"Yuck! It scratched me."

"I told you," said Victor. "Knights taste terrible. Let me cook a big bowl of rabbit stew for you."

"I'm very hungry," said the dragon.

"I don't want to eat a little rabbit.

I want to eat a big knight."

So Viktor tricked the dragon again.

"Try this part of me. It has lots of meat on it."

The dragon grabbed the shield and bit it in half.

"Gross! Something is stuck in my teeth."

"I told you," said Viktor. "Knights taste terrible. Let me bake a sweet carrot cake for you."

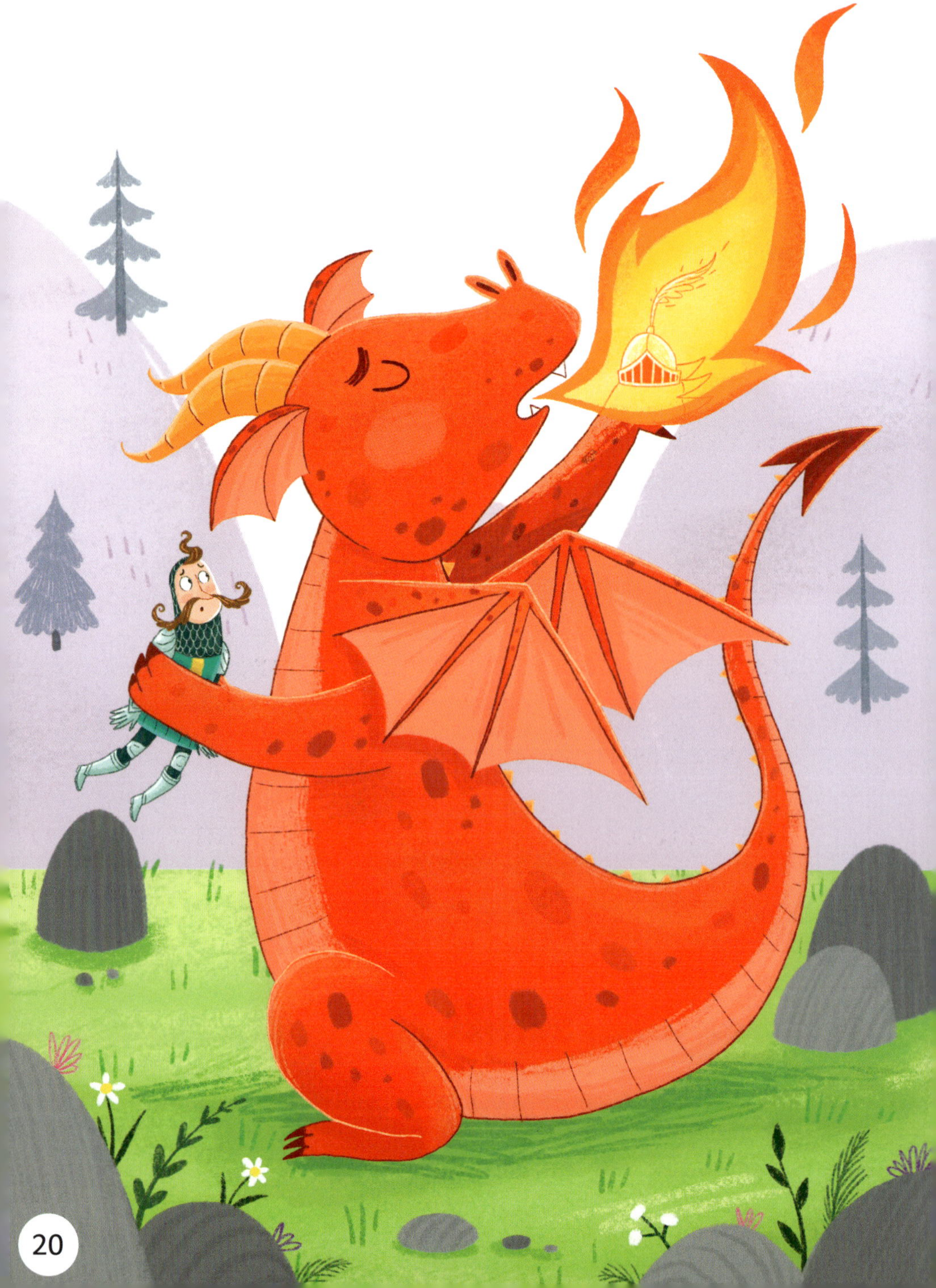

The dragon shook his head. "Today I want to eat a knight sandwich." So Viktor tricked the dragon one more time.

He handed the dragon his helmet. "Heat this up. It will make it softer." The dragon blew fire on the helmet and popped it in his mouth.

"OUCH! It's too hot!"

The dragon was in pain.

"Knights taste terrible!" said the dragon.

"Where is the carrot cake?"

23

"If you don't eat me," said Viktor,

"I will bake a GIANT cake!"

The dragon nodded his head...

while crossing his claws.

Viktor made a big cake.

The dragon ate six slices!

His tummy was full and he fell asleep.

Viktor ran away.

"That was lucky," he said.

So to stop other dragons catching him…

...he became a baker and opened a cake shop.

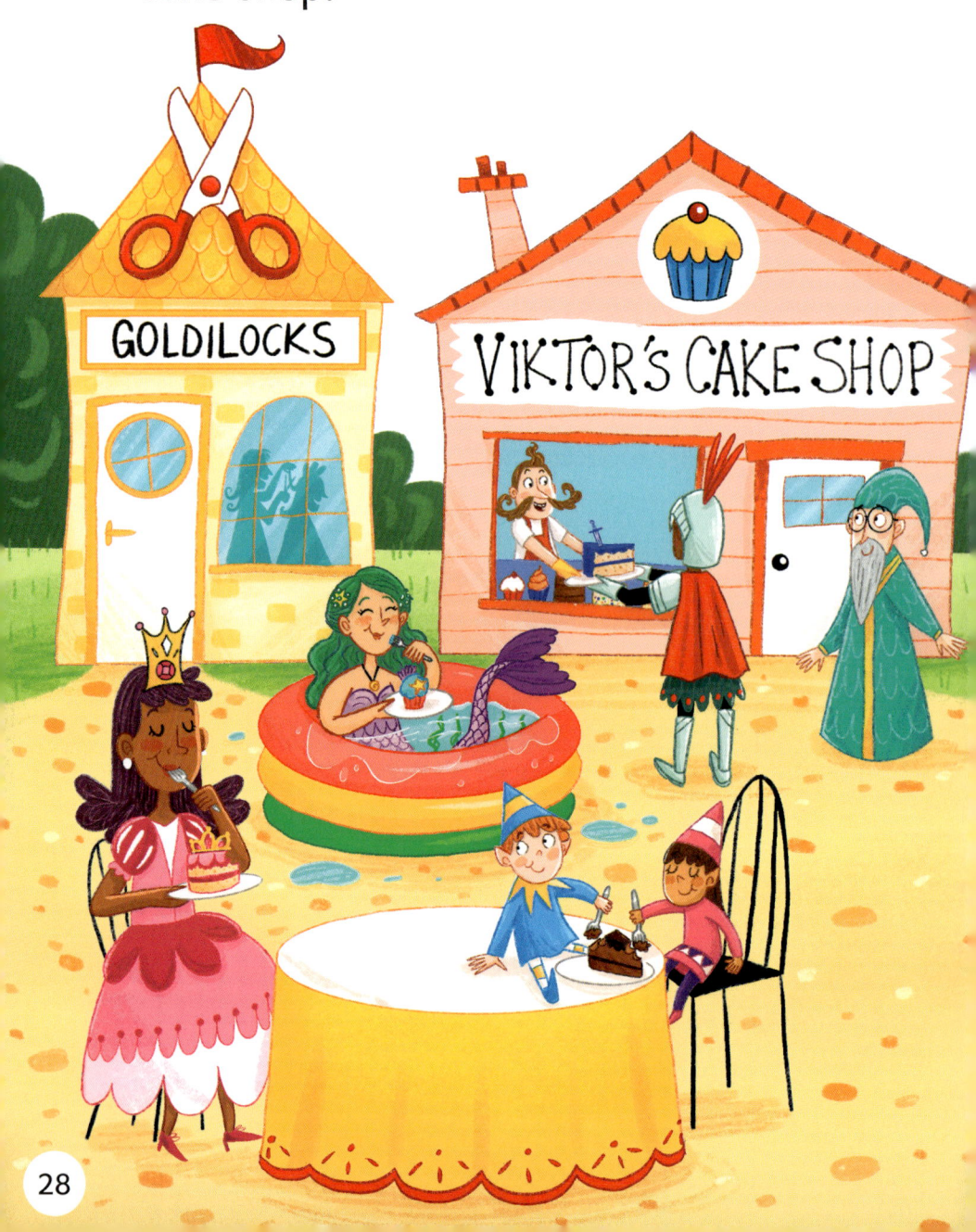

No one ever tried to eat Viktor again because his cakes tasted incredible!

Quiz

1. What kind of soup did Viktor offer the dragon?
a) Potato
b) Chicken
c) Tomato

2. What does the dragon want to eat?
a) Rabbit stew
b) Chicken stew
c) A knight sandwich

3. Why couldn't the dragon eat the helmet?
a) It was too hot
b) It was too spiky
c) It was too hard

4. How many slices of cake did the dragon eat?
a) Five
b) Four
c) Six

5. What is Viktor's new job at the end of the story?
a) Knight
b) Baker
c) Dragon tamer

Turn over for answers

Book Bands for Guided Reading

The Institute of Education book banding system is a scale of colours that reflects the various levels of reading difficulty. The bands are assigned by taking into account the content, the language style, the layout and phonics. Word, phrase and sentence level work is also taken into consideration.

Maverick Early Readers are a bright, attractive range of books covering the pink to white bands. All of these books have been book banded for guided reading to the industry standard and edited by a leading educational consultant.

To view the whole Maverick Readers scheme, visit our website at
www.maverickearlyreaders.com

Or scan the QR code above to view our scheme instantly!

Quiz Answers: 1b, 2c, 3a, 4c, 5b